SO-CFQ-761

BASEBALL
BROTHERS

BASEBALL BROTHERS

by JEFF RUBIN and RICK RAEL

pictures by SANDY KOSSIN

Lothrop, Lee & Shepard Co.
A Division of William Morrow & Co., Inc. • New York

MANHASSET PUBLIC LIBRARY

[BEGINNING
READER]
Rubin

Text copyright © 1976 by Jeff Rubin and Rick Rael.
Illustrations copyright © 1976 by Sandy Kossin.

All rights reserved. No part of this book may be reproduced or utilized in any form or by any means, electronic or mechanical, including photocopying, recording or by any information storage and retrieval system, without permission in writing from the Publisher. Inquiries should be addressed to Lothrop, Lee & Shepard Company, 105 Madison Ave., New York, N.Y. 10016. Printed in the United States of America.   1   2   3   4   5   80   79   78   77   76

Library of Congress Cataloging in Publication Data
Rubin, Jeff. Baseball brothers.
SUMMARY: Two young baseball fans can't get tickets to Henry Aaron's last game of the year, but instead they unexpectedly meet the famous athlete in person. [1. Aaron, Henry,1934-   —Fiction. 2. Baseball—Fiction] I. Rael, Rick, joint author. II. Kossin, Sandy. III. Title. PZ7.R8312Bas [Fic.]   76-3416.
ISBN 0-688-41744-2   ISBN 0-688-51744-7 lib. bdg.

For our friends at the Fifth Street
and Lloyd Street Schools of Milwaukee

James! Hey, James! Come on, get up!

 Hold on, short stuff. I'm coming.

 Well, hurry up or we won't get tickets.

 Slow down, man. The game doesn't start for three hours.

This is Henry's last game this year. Everyone will be there. It's going to be sold out.

 Plenty of time.

 Not unless you get moving.

 Clarence, why are you taking all that junk to the game?

 Junk? What junk?

 With that bat and all, you look like you're going to *play* in the game.

 This is my best bat. I'm
going to ask Henry Aaron
to sign it.

 Now, where are you going to
get next to Henry Aaron?

9

We'll be there early.
We can catch him
before he goes in.

 Aw, man, who cares about him?
I just want to see the game.

 Who cares?! Everyone!
I watch him on TV, and
I have his baseball card.
He is just about the
best player ever.

 Oh, yeah? Then you better
watch him real close.

 What for?

Maybe you'll learn not to strike out all the time.

 Strike out? Me? The way you pitch, I can hit a home run off you any day.

 Are you crazy? Even Hank Aaron couldn't hit off me. I could strike him out on three pitches.

Wha-at?

 Maybe four.

 There you go again, James.
Popping your mouth off,
thinking you're the best
pitcher since Catfish Hunter.
I've never seen any of those
ba–a–ad curves you always
talk about.

 Yeah, well, one day you
ask Catfish Hunter who
showed him his curve ball.
He'll say, "My man,
James 'Curveball' Dixon!"

James, you are too much.
If you showed Catfish
the curve ball, then
I showed Henry Aaron
how to hit.

 OK, short stuff, don't believe
me. What's so great about
Henry Aaron, anyway? Anyone
can hit a home run.

Man, Henry's hit more home runs than anyone. Do you know how many?

 Sure I do.

 How many?

 Seven hundred.

 Oh, man. Don't you know that Henry Aaron has hit over seven hundred and *fifty* home runs?

 If I was the pitcher, he wouldn't hit one.

 You just said anyone can
hit a home run.

 Not off me.

 Come on, James. *I* can hit
one off you.

What! With my ba–a–ad arm? Where's your bat?

 My bat? I can hit your ba-a-ad arm with a toothpick. Let's see that curve ball.

 You sure you want to do this? I don't like making short people look bad.

 Batter up!

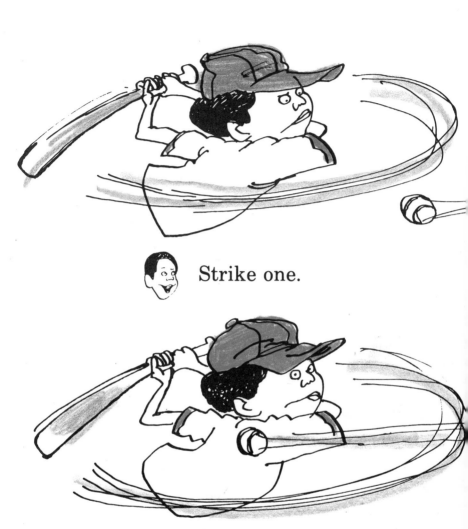

Strike one.

Strike two.

 Strike three!
Better luck next time, kid.
My ups.

Hold on, Curveball. I was
just giving you a break.
So this time when I smash one
over the fence, you won't
feel too bad.

 Little man, you're a story.
But you won't come close to
hitting my curve.

 Let's see that ra–a–ag arm
again.

 OK. Get ready.
Strike one.
Strike two.
Strike three again!

Dog! I never could hit.

Come on, man, you can hit.
But you have to hold the bat
right.

 This is the way
Henry Aaron holds his bat.

 But you're not Henry Aaron.
Don't hold the bat so far
back. Here, like this.

I can't hit.

 Just try it this way.

 Whew-weee! Better look out, James. The next one might take your head off.

Luck! Beginner's luck.

 Hey, here's our bus.
Hurry up!

 I'm coming!

Man, after I see Henry hit, you'll never get that curve by me.

 How come you're so high on Henry? There are plenty of other good players to see.

 James, you don't know anything. Henry Aaron has been playing pro baseball since 1950, when he was sixteen years old.

Sixteen? Wow! Who did he play for?

 A team in the Negro League. The Mobile Bears in Mobile, Alabama. He played shortstop.

 The Negro League? I never heard of that.

In the old days, black players couldn't play in the major leagues. So the guys who wanted to play formed their own teams. And they made a whole league.

 What?

 It's true. Jackie Robinson was the first black man to play in the major leagues. He started in 1949 with the Brooklyn Dodgers.

 How do you know all this stuff?

Man, I *study* all about it.
Ask me anything.

 Well, when did Henry Aaron
get into the major leagues?

He started playing right
field for the Milwaukee
Braves in 1954.

 I thought you said he played
shortstop.

 He did play shortstop, and
second base. But he made too
many errors, so they moved
him to the outfield. And
when the Braves won the World
Series in 1957, Henry was the
Most Valuable Player.

 He must be something.

Yeah. Hammerin' Hank holds
more batting records than
any other player. In 1974
he hit his 715th home run
and broke Babe Ruth's record.
Bad Henry is the home run
king!

Whew-weee! I hope he hits one today!

 Come on, James, let's get our tickets!

Sold out?

 Man! I told you we should have been here early.

 No more tickets!

 After we saved up all summer to see this game. Now we won't see Henry.

 I'll think of something.

 Oh, sure.

 Maybe we can sneak in.

 What?

31

I know how to do it.
Follow me.

 Now!

 You and your great ideas.

 If you didn't have all that junk, we would have made it.

And if you weren't so lazy, we'd have tickets.

 Well, the next time I have a great idea, don't drop that bat on the usher's foot.

 Man, I've *got* to see Henry play. What if we say Henry is our uncle? What if we—

Clarence.

 What if we tell them we're Henry's kids?

 You are crazy. Let's go around to the players' gate. Maybe you can get his autograph.

 Okay.

Nobody here yet. Come on,
man, let's see that bat.
I want to hit one for
Hank Aaron—and Jackie Robinson.

 You sure you want to do this?
I don't like to make tall
people look bad.

 Whew-weee! A home run!

Mister! Hey, mister! Can
you pick up our ball?
Hey, mister!

 James! That's Henry Aaron!
He threw the ball to me!

Now I *know* you are crazy.

 It's him! Come on, man.
And bring my bat!

 Aw, man. Who are all those
people?

I don't know. Let's go ask
him to sign our stuff.

 Mr. Aaron, can I have your
autograph?

Well, we're on . . . sure
you can!

 Clarence is your *number one*
fan, Mr. Aaron. He knows
everything about you! And
I'm your number two fan.
I'm James.

Glad to meet you. So you know all about me?

 Clarence does. Ask him anything.

 Well, let's see. How about this? What's the most home runs I ever hit in one season?

 Aw, everybody knows that. It was 44. Same as your number.

 I told you he knows everything!

 He sure does. Now all those people watching know it too!

What?!

 James, we're on TV!

 Oh, man!

It's been nice talking
to you, fellows. But you'd
better go on in.

 Well, Mr. Aaron, we don't
have tickets for the game.

Why not?

 They were all sold out
when we got here.

 Hmmm. Say, how would you
TV guys like some new faces
up in the booth?

Us?

 Gentlemen, meet Clarence and James, the "Baseball Brothers." They're all-stars, on and off the field. How about it?

 Good idea! Who knows, maybe they can tell us something we don't know about Henry Aaron. Come on, fellows.

 You hear the man, don't you?

 We sure do!

 Wow! Thanks, Mr. Aaron!

Let's go. Air time in
ten minutes.

Hey, Clarence.

 What?

 I told you I'd think of something!